P9-BUH-878

AN ADDISONIAN PRESS BOOK

First published in the United States in 1976, by Addison-Wesley.

Printed in Great Britain.

All rights reserved. No part of this book may be reproduced in
any form without written permission from
Addison-Wesley Publishing Company, Inc., Reading,
Massachusetts 01867.

First printing.

ISBN: 0-201-06245-3   LCN: 75-15314

First published by Penguin Books Ltd.

Little Gray Neck

a Russian folktale retold by

JAMES RIORDAN AND EILEEN COLWELL

ILLUSTRATED BY CAROLINE SHARPE

▲ ADDISON-WESLEY

It was autumn and the birds were getting ready for their long, long journey to a warmer country where they would spend the winter.

The big birds – the swans, geese and ducks – set about their preparations calmly, but the small birds – snipe, lapwings and sandpipers – chattered and fussed and flapped.

"What's all this fuss about?" snorted Father Drake. "We'll all fly away in good time. There's no sense in dashing hurry-scurry along the river bank from dawn to dusk!"

The time came for the Duck family to get ready, but little Gray Neck could not go. A fox had hurt her before Mother Duck could beat him off with her strong wings.

Every day it grew colder. The trees changed color and a keen wind blew. The young birds flew a little further each day to prepare for the journey, but Gray Neck could only watch, unable to fly.

"How sad to leave her behind!" said Mother Duck to her husband. "We shall fly south to the sun while she, poor dear, will stay here and freeze."

"Don't be so upset," said the Drake. He loved Gray Neck too, of course, and it was sad to leave her, but what else could they do?

Early one morning while the mist still lay over the river, the birds' leaders cried "Time to go!"

First to take wing were the marsh birds. Then the cranes, the swans and the geese. Last of all Father Drake rose into the air and the other ducks followed him.

Only Mother Duck stayed behind for a moment to say goodbye to little Gray Neck.

"I don't want to leave you," she sighed. "I love you dearly. But it is my duty to go with the other children."

"You will be back in the spring, won't you, Mother?" asked Gray Neck anxiously.

"Yes, of course, my dear child," said Mother Duck. "Farewell." She rose into the air to fly after the other birds.

"I shall think of you all the time!" cried Gray Neck. She watched her mother grow smaller and smaller in the sky.

Now she was all alone. How she missed her family. The forest was silent. At night the river froze close to the bank, but in the morning it melted again. "Will the whole river turn to ice?" wondered the little duck. This was her first winter, and she did not know what would happen.

One day Gray Neck left the water and wandered into the forest. There she met a Hare.

"How you scared me!" panted the Hare. "My heart jumped into my mouth. What are you doing here? Don't you know that all the ducks flew away days ago?"

"I cannot fly," said Gray Neck. "The Fox broke my wing."

"That Fox! There is no worse beast in the forest," said the Hare. "He has been after me for ages, and in winter there is nowhere to hide. I wish I were a duck. Even though you cannot fly, you can swim. It is safer on the water, but watch out when it freezes over. That's when the Fox will be on the prowl."

Soon the first snow fell and the river froze in the daytime as well as at night. The ice crept silently across the river until it was only in the middle that the water ran swiftly. There Gray Neck was safe.

One day the Fox came slinking to the bank. "Ah, my little friend," he said, "good day to you."

"*Please* go away!" cried the duck, trembling with fear.

"Is that what I get for my politeness?" said the Fox. "You don't want to believe all you hear about me. Farewell, I'll see you again soon!"

When the Fox had gone, the Hare came out of the forest.

"Be careful, Gray Neck," he said. "The Fox will come back again. You must never leave the water."

Now the ground was all covered over with a snow-white carpet and the trees glistened with frost. At night the wolves howled in the forest.

One morning the Fox returned. "I've missed you, little duck," he said. "Come over here to the bank, or I'll come out to you." He stepped onto the ice, but it cracked. He had to go away.

Every day the Fox came back to see if the river had frozen over. Every day the duck's pool of water grew smaller. Gray Neck tried to hide by diving again and again.

The Hare watched timidly from the forest. "That wicked Fox will get Gray Neck soon, I'm afraid."

One cold morning the Hare and his friends were frisking about, slapping their furry paws together to keep warm.

Suddenly an old hunter on skis came through the snow. When he saw the hares he was pleased. "They will make my old woman a nice warm fur coat," he said and fired his gun.

But the hares had seen him in time. "Scatter, brothers!" they cried and they escaped into the forest.

"I'll get you one day, you cross-eyed hares!" grumbled the hunter. "The old woman must have her fur coat. She told me not to come back without it."

He looked towards the river and caught sight of the Fox on the ice. The Fox was crawling nearer and nearer to the terrified Gray Neck. But the old man was too far away to see the duckling and he exclaimed in delight: "There's the old woman's fur coat again! I must shoot carefully – the old woman will beat me if the collar is full of holes."

BANG! He fired. There was a flurry of snow and the hunter ran to the edge of the ice to pick up the Fox. Instead of a fox he found a frightened little duck swimming frantically on a tiny patch of water.

"Bless me!" cried the old man. "That's the first time I've seen a fox turn into a duck. What a cunning creature he is!"

"Well, that's the end of my old woman's fur coat once again," grumbled the old man. "What are you doing here, you silly little thing? And how did you break your wing?"

"Oh dear, oh dear," sighed the old man. "You'll either freeze to death or the Fox will get you." He stood silent, shaking his head.

Then he said: "I'll tell you what I'll do. I'll take you along for my granddaughter, Masha. She will be pleased. In the spring you can lay eggs for my old woman and hatch some ducklings for her. What do you say to that?"

Gray Neck said nothing, but she let the old man pick her up and put her under his warm coat.

"We won't tell the old woman I missed the Fox and the hares," said the old man as he went across the snow. "Her fur coat must walk about the forest a little longer."

At the door of their hut his wife and Masha were waiting for him. "I've something for you," said the old man and he opened his coat and showed them Gray Neck.

"Ah ha! now we shall have some duck eggs," said the old woman, forgetting her fur coat for the moment.

Masha took Gray Neck in her arms and stroked the little duck's feathers. "Oh, how sweet she is!" the little girl said softly.

Gray Neck quacked with pleasure. "Now the cruel Fox will not be able to catch me," the duck thought contentedly.

So the old man and the old woman and Masha and Gray Neck lived happily together all the long cold winter.